SECRET SANTA MURDERS

Short and Strange Stories for the Holiday Season

Chris Parks, Megan Johnson, Mandy Kerr

PFL Artist Books

CONTENTS

SECRET SANTA MURDERS

By Chris Parks

Gerald twisted in his chair, stretching his back out. A familiar squeak greeted him as the old chair protested at its maltreatment. He glanced at the clock. Twenty minutes left of work. Of course, Gerald did not need to be here. At seventy he was past retirement age, but he liked getting up for work in the morning, the routine, the feeling useful. There seemed no point in retiring. Margaret, his ex-wife, had disagreed, she had a plan. The dreaded garden remodel, like Mrs Miggins' monstrosity at number twenty-three, but with more "opulence" Margaret had said. Arthur Miggins slipped a disk installing the cascading water feature, resulting in a week's stay in hospital; rumour was down The Admiral that he had begged to be kept in longer, citing insanity…hers, not his. Gerald didn't fancy that much; Gerald liked the garden as it was. Simple and plain; a nice place for a cup of tea on a summer evening where he could listen to birdsong or next-door shout at each other. On one occasion he even heard them making up, a fact that had ruined the garden for him for a couple of weeks. He didn't want a water feature or raised beds. He disliked plants and flowers that he couldn't pronounce the names of. There was a reason Latin was a dead language. They had argued about it with increasing regularity. She had called him "boring" and "lacking imagination". She had asked a local gardener to "price up" the job without his knowledge. Three months later Margaret ran off with him; like Lady Chatterley's lover, but with tattoos and a perma-tan. The first thing that Gerald noticed when she had gone, was how peaceful life was. He could pop in The Admiral for a quiet pint without having to report in first or watch the snooker or…well anything he wanted to do.

The chatter from the rest of the office was a comforting hum. Rain gently drummed on the window next to him, the droplets competing in a race to reach the bottom of the pane. The watery trails left behind softened the colourful, bright lights from the houses nearby. A ten-foot Santa flashed brightly for a moment, waving, before vanishing into the darkness. A heartbeat later a warm white snowman appeared tipping his hat, then Rudolph with his bright red nose. The opening notes of "We Wish You a Merry Christmas" could be heard as the festive lights covering the whole house danced merrily along in time with the music. Gerald wasn't feeling very festive. The cold had got into his gammy knee and people were generally being irritatingly cheerful. The queen of the irritatingly cheerful now stood and was tinging a bottle with a pen. She addressed the office.

'Evening all!' Gerald's toes curled in at the sound of her voice. "Thank you for bringing in your Secret Santa pressies on time.' The i in time was elongated with an attempted faux cheerfulness, however, it tended to give her more of an insincere undertone.

'Darren and I will be handling them out in five.' Dazza hated being called Darren, Gerald thought. Harriett Most was the only person who did, and she put the emphasis on "REN". Dazza shuddered and caught Gerald's eye.

Harriett Most was a force to be reckoned with. Her neatly permed hair with its lilac tint certainly set her apart from most sixty-something-year-olds. A faint scent of Parma violets was her usual calling card, lingering around for some time after she had left. Her eyes, were pale blue, surrounded by thick, black-rimmed glasses. Her clothing was predominantly floral, although Gerald did remember a butterfly print outfit that was a garish assault on the eyes. Gerald knew that she had been married three times. Her last ex-husband, Desmond, worked up on the third floor in accounting. He was a tired-looking man with unkempt hair, which Gerald thought was strange as he was certain that it was a wig. The end of his nose was permanently red, and he sniffed a lot. Desmond knew that Gerald worked with Harriett and had offered the information freely.

Gerald had wished that he had stopped there...he hadn't. He went on to tell him that the reason for the divorce was that he couldn't keep up with her..."in the biblical sense, if you know what I mean". He had winked and nudged Gerald. Gerald knew what he meant; Desmond had been as subtle as a lobbed house brick. Gerald felt appalled by the confession. In part because of the salacious way Desmond imparted the information, it felt grubby, too personal for a man he hardly knew. The other part was that since he'd separated from his wife, Gerald had been on Harriett's radar. Gerald was the first to admit he wasn't the most perceptive of fellows when it came to the language of love; he had missed the subtle clues, the touching of the arm, the playing with her hair around him, the coy sideways glances. He even dismissed these as a ridiculous notion when Dazza pointed them out. Harriett oversaw scheduling the break times. They started to share an unusual amount of them. Gerald even managed to dismiss this as pure coincidence. Then at last year's office Secret Santa draw, he pulled her name out of the hat...and he was sure she pulled his. The gift, a pair of novelty underpants with hearts on them came with some subtle comments which led him to believe that they came from her. Dazza reckoned she had rigged it. Gerald conceded he was probably right, especially as he had drawn her again this year.

'You got her a too nice a present last year, it looked like too much effort', said Dazza, referring to the vase he had given her last year. In truth, it was a vase that had sat at the back of a cupboard, still in its box, for many years. It hadn't felt like he had made an effort, especially "the too much effort" that Dazza was referring to. This year he decided to make it very clear that very little effort had been made. On his way home he stopped off at the 50p and £1 shop on the high street. It was definitely the worst shop on the high street. The shopfront, painted gaudy pink, now peeling off in large flakes, revealing a reddish undercoat, the overall effect looked like the pox. Inside the floor was sticky with God knows what and there was a permanent smell of stale beer and tobacco. The owner, Harvey Kite, sat entrenched by the front door like Cerberus at the gates of Hell. Rumour had it that his shop had never been successfully shoplifted. Whether this was because the shop was full of tat and not worth nicking or because the last person to try was clotheslined by Harvey's tree trunk arm as they tried to run for it, resulting in a neck brace and a year's worth of physio to be able to walk straight again. His ample posterior perched on a tiny stool that, Gerald considered, was not fit for purpose, although it was stoic in its attempt, like Atlas holding the world on his shoulders. His, used-to-be white shirt, ketchup stained with the old cigarette burns dotted around it was his uniform. Gerald approached the counter.

'Evening Harvey, got anything good for a Christmas present for a lady?'

Harvey didn't even look up from his newspaper or remove the cigarette from his mouth.

'Is there a romantic entanglement?'

'Oh no, far from it,' said Gerald. 'Actually, trying to have the opposite effect, you know…put the lady off, as it were.'

Harvey sniffed and reached under the counter, lifting a yellow duck in a pink box.

'That'll do you, fresh in from the Orient, exotic'

'What is it?' Gerald asked, wondering if he should have been able to guess.

'Bath Bomb…in the shape of a duck.' Harvey shrugged his shoulders, 'Ladies love a bath bomb, don't they?'

He looked up at Gerald, daring him to challenge this insight into the female psyche. In truth, Harvey Kite considered himself quite the lothario. He was a popular member of an online chat group. A steady stream of ladies vied for his attention. The addition of Chris Hemsworth with his top off as his profile picture seemed to increase this attention. He was rather pleased with himself.

'Umm I guess,' Gerald gave a little chuckle that only the truly unsure give. 'Seems perfect…I'll take it.'

'That'll be one pound fifty. No returns allowed for discolouration of bathroom equipment or skin irritations…'

Gerald hesitated for a heartbeat, then placed one pound fifty on the countertop.

'I thought everything was supposed to cost one pound or fifty pence?'

Harvey Kite pointed to the half-broken shop sign. 'It says 50p and a £1, Tha's one pound fifty innit?'

Gerald rolled his eyes; he couldn't argue with the man's logic, although he felt like he had been outmanoeuvred by a grubby sloth. Gerald raised his hand in defeat and left the shop. He had forgotten how cold it was outside and the wind bit hard as a reminder. He walked down the street towards the supermarket. A red sports car drove past a little faster than it should have done. Dirty water sprayed up Gerald's beige trousers. He cursed the driver under his breath, then when they were further away, a little louder. He noticed the licence plate GR36ORY and recognised this as his boss's son's car.

Gregory Danvers was, for want of a better word, a man-child; spoilt, selfish and arrogant. His father, Gary Danvers, had built his insurance company up from scratch. He was a straight talker and expected a shift from his staff, but Gerald liked him. He would always put his hand in his pocket to buy a round of drinks on the office outings and his wife Deidre knew when everyone's birthday was and would send in her speciality lemon drizzle cake. Gerald didn't like lemon drizzle cake, thinking it overrated as a cake; but he appreciated the sentiment. He followed Gregory into the shop, still miffed about his damp legs and feeling like an apology was needed.

The bright lights of the shop momentarily dazzled Gerald, however, the warmth was a welcome relief from the gnawing cold. He went straight to the gift wrap aisle, noting that Gregory was just leaving the other end towards home baking. Gerald grabbed some coffee and a couple of pork chops for dinner. Gregory was just finishing at the till and spotted Gerald.

'Graham, isn't it? You work for me Dad don't you?'

'Gerald,' Gerald corrected, 'Yeah, I do, Customer service.'

'Yeah, whatever. What happened to you? You look like you are covered in shite.'

'Well, you did. When you drove past…going too fast, you splashed me.'

Gregory laughed. It was a scratchy little laugh. He showed no remorse.

'Should have got out the way then mate. You need aisle eight, the one with the washing powder on it. Maybe get some Vanish stain remover as well.'

Gregory turned and walked off towards the exit still shaking his head and laughing. Gerald went to go after him, to continue the conversation until he felt vindicated. Then he remembered that he still had not paid for his shopping. He put his shopping on the till and the checkout girl gave him a pitiful smile. He felt a proper grump.

The glass was tinged again as Gerald unwrapped his Secret Santa gift. A pair of socks/brief set with a picture of a phone on them and the phrase "I think you're texty" on them. Gerald sighed.

DCI Bill Sagers was fed up. It was cold, rainy and dinner time. He had an ache in his belly that was about to be solved with a donner from Harry's Kebab when his phone rang.

'It's a weird one,' the call handler said, 'Right up your street Bill, you can thank me later.'

'Thanks mate, what're the details?'

'Woman in her sixties, carked it while on her webcam, from what looked like an anaphylactic reaction. The thing is, before she dies, with her final breath, she accuses someone of murdering her.'

Bill sucked in air through his teeth and let out a long sigh. They always gave him the weird ones. Last month it was the Amorous Chicken Fancier, the month before that was the Sausage Roll Guy, and he didn't even want to think about Mittens and the Stew Saga; which nearly put him off his mother's home-cooked meals forever.

'The witnesses are still, well, still there, if you get me?' the voice crackled from the speaker. Bill was sure that he didn't. They were either there or they weren't. He rang the doorbell of number seven.

The smell of Parma Violet was the first thing that Bill noticed. It felt like it was everywhere, the carpet, the walls, even the light in the hallway seemed to be infused with it. It seemed to stick in the bridge of his nose, stinging slightly; he wanted to sneeze. Think about pineapples, he thought. He remembered reading somewhere that if you thought about pineapples then it stopped you from sneezing. So far it had worked, a triumph of mind over matter, he always considered. A uniformed officer stepped out of the room at the end.

'She's in here sir.'

Bill stuck his head around the door. The flash from the forensic photographer's camera momentarily took his sight, leaving a ring of bright light in his vision. As he tried to blink his eyes back to normality, they settled on the body in the chair. The woman's face was distorted as if it was a caricature. Abnormally large eyes bulged behind thick-rimmed glasses, her lips looked like fat slugs, her swollen tongue, discoloured blue poked out through lipstick-stained teeth. For a moment Bill thought that even her hair had been affected, then realised that it was a rinse dye. The negligee she was wearing was trying its best to offer some decency, with only a modicum of success.

'Harriett Most,' said the officer, 'Three witnesses watched her die; one of them..erm…Mammasboy42 called it in.'

The officer could tell from the puzzled look on Bill's face that this needed more explanation.

'She was a cam girl, Sir. We still have the three witnesses online for you to talk to. Babyboyroy and Lilrascal are the other two. There was a fourth, but they left PDQ when she snuffed it. Roy said they were called BabyG. Takes all sorts, I guess.' He motioned to the TV screen on the dresser in front of the body. Bill turned to see three older gentlemen, one of whom he was sure was wearing a baby blue onesie; the name Mammasboy42 was in the top left corner in red. Bill looked at his colleague for, well…he wasn't sure; he was answered with a shrug.

'Who can tell me what happened?' he ventured.

Babyboyroy spoke first, his voice gruff and it quivered slightly with genuine emotion.

'It was our usual Friday night nursery session with Momma Slocombe and she offered to make it Christmas-themed and open some pressies for us. We were so excited.'

'She had one that had some Cwissmas…I mean Christmas cake in it from work,' Lilrascal interjected. 'She unwrapped it for us and ate it in a seductive manner.' The last word choked off as a tear rolled down his scarlet cheek.

Mammasboy42 continued, 'She started to cough at first, then choke and went a funny colour.'

'You said she was murdered?'

'Well, with her final gasp, she said, "Gerald, he's murdered me" And then she just lay there gurgling for a few seconds, then… dead.'

Bill took a moment to process this, then looked at the officer.

'Take their names, real ones mind. Do we know who Baby G is? Do we know who Gerald is?'

'Babyboyroy said she mentioned a Gerald at work, said that he was her Secret Santa, might have who the gift was from. Baby G, G for Gerald maybe?'

Bill scratched his chin 'That is a bit of a coincidence, isn't it?'

'Dead, what do you mean dead?' Gerald was confused.

'Dead, as in as a doornail, pushing up daisies, she is no more!' said Dazza with a little more enthusiasm than was probably needed.

'But she was in yesterday, she was fine then…are you sure?'

'Positive mate. Des on the third floor told me this morning. Rumour has it that she had an allergic reaction to something, anaphylactic shock or something he called it. He said it was her Secret Santa pressie or something…you all right mate?'

Gerald felt the chill spread through his body as his blood ran cold. He steadied himself on the wall, his heart thumped hard in his chest.

'I was her Secret Santa! The present was from me! What have I done?' Gerald's voice trailed off at the end.

'Jeez, what have you done? What did you get her? You know she has allergies n' stuff!' Dazza said.

'Just a bath thing from Harvey Kite's store, I…I didn't mean to hurt her, I…I didn't mean to kill her!'

'Mate, his stuff is toxic at the best of times. Can't believe you done her in!'

Gerald looked up at Dazza, he was appalled. Had he killed her? Was this all his fault? He tried in vain to find a way to defend himself, but he couldn't find one. He opened his mouth to speak but was interrupted by a voice down the other end of the office. A tall, unkempt man in an un-ironed shirt, flanked by two police officers was talking to Gregory Danvers.

'We are looking for Gerald Plimpton. Can you tell us where he is?'

'You probably mean Graham', Danvers replied. 'He works somewhere down that way'. He pointed in the direction of Gerald. 'What is this about? The old tart who snuffed it?'

'We are not at liberty to discuss an ongoing investigation. Did you know her well?'

' She was a bit of a busybody, always up in people's business, if you know what I mean?'

'I am sure I don't, enlighten me,' replied Bill, his curiosity starting to show a mild interest in Gregory Danvers. A guilty mind would often unwittingly give away all sorts of information and Gregory Danvers was probably guilty of something. He was well-known to the local law enforcement officers. A litany of petty crimes and civil disorders ranging from drunk and disorderly, criminal damage and drug possession probably tipped the iceberg, but having a rich dad meant that not many charges stuck and it galled Bill that he was still walking around free as you like.

'Well….you know…always asking questions, acting like she knows everything. Someone probably done her in.' Bill noticed a bead of sweat escape from Gregory's hairline and roll slowly down his temple. 'Me ma said she didn't trust her one bit.'

'Care to elaborate?' Bill chided himself. His tone was slightly more accusational than he had meant it to be and he saw Gregory clam up; his usual cockiness returned.

'Nah, I ain't doing your job for you copper.' He turned and walked off laughing, Bill sighed.

Gerald steadied himself on the wall, watching in horror as the policemen talked to Gregory Danvers, their voices sounded muffled and distant like he was underwater. Dazza was talking to him, however, the words didn't compute to anything sensible. The wall he was leaning up against felt like it was moving, pushing him closer to the opposite wall. He tried to breathe but he felt like the air had been sucked out of the room. Was the office always this small? You can't swing a cat, his mother would have said, bless her. The office felt like a prison cell. A prison cell…the word rattled around his head and settled on the amygdala, the simple part of the brain that controls fight or flight. It felt his fear and prepared its pre-flight checklist. His heart rate increased, his pupils dilated, adrenaline flooded his body. It is said that anxiety is caused by this primitive response. The amygdala cannot tell the difference between standing in front of a crowd to give a speech and being chased by a dinosaur. Sometimes it overreacts. Gerald's had just decided that this was a very big dinosaur indeed. His feet were moving before he could register their movement. He had no idea where he was running to in that moment, only that the running seemed important. He nearly tripped over the cleaner's vacuum cleaner as he shot past and down the back stairs. The cleaner shook their head in disgust. Dazza watched him go, stunned at the speed of the old man. He caught the cleaner's eye, then a thought occurred to him, a memory of sorts. One of those moments in life that only seems odd after the fact, coupled with new information. He scratched his chin thoughtfully.

Bill approached the man standing there gawping at the cleaner. He was tall, wearing a black turtleneck jumper. A thick gold chain was worn on the outside of the neck of the jumper and his hair was slicked back with a little too much hair gel. He smelt like cheap aftershave, something called Hai Karate or Blue Stratos probably. It reminded him of the punters in the betting shop where he grew up in the seventies.

'Gerald Plimpton?'

'Nah mate, Dazza Cooper.' He held out his hand, Bill didn't take it. 'Gerald was here a minute ago, but he had to shoot off; he wasn't feeling well. Had some bad news he did.'

'You mean about Harriett Most? Was he close to her?'

'Yeah, I told him she had gone to the great handbag shop in the sky and then he saw you and…well just legged it.'

'And you didn't think that was suspicious?' Bill was getting exasperated now. 'Which way did he go?'

'Well now you mention it he did say something about killing her.'

Bill glared at him, expecting more but the man infuriatingly just stood there with a lopsided grin on his face, like he was auditioning to fill the post of village idiot.

Gerald sat at the corner table in The Admiral Pub, the third shot of whiskey had started to settle his nerves, although Burt was still looking at him with curiosity. His shaggy head turned from side to side and his ears flopped gently over each time. He gave a little whine and then laid down next to the log fire, a little disappointed the human hadn't saved him a crisp; soon he was dreaming of squirrels.

Gerald had no idea what to do. He was aware that running

away probably wasn't the greatest life choice. He should probably hand himself in and face the consequences. His rationale was that he hadn't meant to kill her and that had to go towards something, didn't it? His phone vibrated on the tablet in front of him and he could see it was Dazza calling. He went to answer the call, but the phone flashed up low battery and unceremoniously powered off.

Dazza was a bit miffed, he just wanted to help his mate out, but the copper had been really off-hand with him. He went back to his cubical to sulk and to make matters worse, because Gerald had run off, he had to do the late shift on his own. He looked around to see if anyone else was still there, but everyone else had left for the day except the cleaning lady hoovering a few workstations away. The earlier thought came back to him fully processed by his subconscious working some serious overtime in the background. He picked up his phone and dialled. Gerald's number rang and then went to voicemail.

'Hello, mate listen...just had a thought. I think I saw Danvers switching the tags on the Secret Santa presents the other day. Thought they looked suspicious, Speak later.' Dazza ended the call. He felt good, he liked Gerald and hated the thought that he might be a murderer. He also felt like he needed a pee. Best go now he thought before it gets busy, he thought. He went up to the toilet on the next floor, mostly because it still had the tropical air freshener and not the lemon one. If he shut his eyes, he could be on a lovely tropical island with a pina colada cocktail and the sand beneath his feet.

When he returned to his station there was a box on his desk with a note that read "Happy Birthday Dazza!" He looked at the box, it wasn't his birthday till the weekend, but he wasn't about to complain. He lifted the lid off the box. Inside was a slice of cake, a bit like a cherry bakewell. Dazza lifted it, looked around, sat down and then took a couple of big bites. Within seconds he felt his chest tighten. He tried to breathe but his lungs felt paralyzed; he pulled at his shirt collar, attempting to loosen it but his hand was shaking too much. A searing pain spread through his head was the last feeling he had. His body convulsed for a moment or two more and then he was still, slumped in his chair.

Gary Danver sat in his Range Rover and breathed out a long sigh. In some ways, Harriett's death solved some problems, however, some problems remained. There was compromising material in her emails for instance, which was why he was trying to log in to her account on his laptop. He could just ask IT to reset it but that would arouse suspicion and he couldn't afford any more mistakes; he had been sloppy and careless already, but now he was taking the opportunity to tidy it all up. No fuss, no sordid scandals, neat and tidy, although his boy might still be a problem that needed dealing with, a problem for later he thought. It was no use. He couldn't access the emails and now it had locked him out for half an hour. The knot in his stomach tightened again, He always believed the bowel was an emotional organ, reflecting how you really feel under the calm persona you portray; like a swan's palmated feet furiously peddling under the water while the rest of the swan is serene on the surface. He looked in the rear-view mirror and straightened his tie, I am a swan, he thought to himself; and he hoped Deidrie wouldn't divorce him.

Bill was fed up, his main suspect had fled before he could question him, forensics had come back and confirmed arsenic poisoning as the cause of death, he wanted to access the woman's emails, but the IT company had demanded a warrant first; that would take time. The only saving grace was that security had given him a copy of Gerald Plimpton's ID photo, so at least he knew who he was looking for. The wrapping paper the Secret Santa present had come in was exclusive to Sainsbury's. He asked one of the uniformed officers, PC Pembroke, to pop to the local one to check the CCTV, maybe that would throw up some new information. Right now, he was hungry, thirsty and his feet ached. He looked up and down the high street, among the boutique coffee shops and tanning salons, he saw a sign that said home-cooked food. A good old-fashioned pub with its white-painted walls and black-painted trims. The sign showed an important man with medals and a tricorn hat; the words above said The Admiral. Maybe a cheeky half would be ok, he thought.

Gerald had decided that his best course of action would be to claim that it was an accidental death. If it wasn't premeditated then it couldn't be murder, just a simple accident. No life terms or anything. To prove this, he would need to speak to Harvey Kite who could confirm that the offending item was brought at his suggestion. If he was quick, he could get to the shop before it closed at nine.

Sometimes, Bill thought, to be a good copper, you needed a modicum of hard work, a pinch of common sense, an eye for detail, but mostly an abundance of pure unadulterated dumb luck. The point in case right now. He had lost his prime suspect; however, his natural biorhythms had led to a need that required to be fulfilled; hunger and thirst, coupled together with an ache in his feet and an almost pathological avoidance of anything vaguely hipster; dumb luck. He looked at the photo ID that had been given to him by the security department and again at the man sitting at the table at the other end of the pub. Bill sipped his half of bitter and contemplated his next move, determined that his next move would happen after he finished his drink.

Harvey Kite did one last check of the stock room door to make sure it was locked. A rip-off Peppa Pig toy call Peggy Porker suddenly sprang to life, uttering her catchphrase "Jorge, you are doing it all wrong!", startling him. He turned quickly but nothing was there.

'Hello? Anybody there? I am just about to close.' He stood perfectly still for a moment, listening intently. If it was that Haslet kid, with the wonky eye, who has been hanging around outside all day; then he would gut him. No one stole from Harvey Kite. He slowly moved towards the front door. Behind him a tin rolled across the floor, he spun as quickly as he could and froze.

'Get out of here you little shite, I know your mum and dad!' He moved towards the front of the shop again, towards the door; corner the bugger, he thought, no way past. He reached under the counter for his baseball bat, however, it wasn't there, must have rolled further back he thought. He risked a glance under the countertop to check, instantly realising his mistake. It all happened within seconds, the hurried footsteps, the little whoosh of air then the sickening thud as the bat connected with his skull. Curiously, he couldn't tell if the cracking sound was his skull splitting in two or the bat snapping in half; it was after all from his own stock of baseball bats and, therefore inferior in every possible way. Oh well, he thought, if you live on the edge, you are not likely to die in your bed; shouldn't have gotten involved with the Danvers lot though; his unremarkable life slipped away as the figure watched him for a moment and then exited the shop.

Bill watched as the elderly man, known to him as Gerald Plimpton, suddenly sprang to his feet with a swiftness that belied his age, startling the sleeping dog by the fire. It gave a little "Woof" of annoyance before resuming his apathetic torpor. Bill necked the rest of his half, watching as Gerald darted out the side door at the other end of the pub. He thanked the barmaid and left by the same exit. He tried to remember all the training they had had about trailing a potentially violent suspect, but all he could remember was not to follow too closely; and don't look them in the eye... but that might be dangerous animals. He put his hands in his pockets in an attempt to look nonchalant, with the added benefit that it also stopped the evening chill gnawing at his fingertips. He could see Gerald weaving his way through the remaining shoppers taking advantage of the late-night shopping hours, he seemed to be a man on a mission Bill thought, gathering pace to keep up with the man. His phone rang in his pocket, but there was no time to answer, he was doing proper coppering, they would have to wait.

He was now matching the older man's pace, meandering his way past the shoppers, who seemed oblivious to the drama unfolding around them. Cat and mouse, Bill thought, or maybe that was being too dramatic. In truth, he wasn't sure if he was supposed to be the cat or the mouse. A car horn blared from near the entrance to the supermarket; Bill glanced over to see a red sports car cutting up a blue Peugeot, before revving off into the car park. He turned his attention back to his quarry, the white halo of hair on Gerald's head making it easy to see him, even as he approached a larger crowd exiting a nearby coffee shop, they passed between him and Gerald. All of Bill's focus was directed towards the thrill of the chase. He didn't see the mobility scooter entering stage left until it was too late; the front wheel rolling over his toes and the chassis colliding with his knee, stopping him dead in his tracks. His yelp of pain was drowned out by the barrage of verbal abuse from the shrivelled prune at the controls of the scooter. His attempt at apology was meant with a sharp crack across the arm from the old lady's walking stick. He stepped back and she zoomed off at speed. He made a mental note to check the legal speed limit for such a vehicle. He looked back down the street, attempting to reorientate himself on Gerlad's head...but it was gone. He scanned either side of the street, the orange glow from the streetlamps giving a warming effect on the passersby. There were no roads to turn off into; so, reasoned Bill, Gerald must have gone into one of the shops. He quickened his pace looking for a likely destination, dismissing the knitting shop and the cake shop, both looking closed. The bookies was across the road and well-lit, Bill was sure he would be able to see Gerald there and he couldn't. So, within the few seconds range, when Bill had taken his eyes off Gerald, it could only be either the Fifty Pence and a Pound shop or the Ann Summers shop. Something told Bill that Gerald wasn't the see-thru nightie, fluffy handcuffs type. In earnest, he refocused his attention towards the shabby shop full of tat.

Gerald had an odd thought, well, odd given the circumstances. This was the most amount of blood he had ever seen. He certainly couldn't think of a time when there was more. The previous record was held by Timothy Marchant in nineteen fifty-nine. Timothy was prone to nosebleeds and one time during story time he had a gusher, proper streaming like something out of a horror movie. That was a lot of blood; a drop in the ocean compared to the flood emitting from Harvey's head right now. Later, Gerald would reflect on the fact that this was the first dead body he had ever seen, however now, it was all about the blood, so much blood. He felt nausea rise at the back of his throat. He turned away and vomited the contents of his stomach...over a pair of slightly worn brown leather shoes. He looked up to see the annoyance and disgust on the face of the unkept detective he had seen earlier talking to Gregory.

'Sorry' he managed to mutter before the bile reached his throat again, He retched again but the detective had the good sense to move out of the way this time.

Gary Danvers turned the radio off but kept the engine running. It was bitterly cold outside, he felt like he needed the warmth. The orange glow from the Sainsbury's sign was becoming blurred by the small droplets of sleet now lying gently on the windows. He was contemplating life. He felt like he was losing control. The knot in his stomach felt unnatural and cumbersome. His phone started to ring, the caller showed his wife's name. It was the tenth time she had called in the last hour. The shame he felt, the coldness, the mire he was sinking into, despair seemed too gentler a word for how he felt. He couldn't look Deidre in the eyes since she came home early the other day; and the boy, why did he have to be with her? He would never let it go. Gary knew he needed to act. Get ahead of the situation; Gregory needed to be dealt with. A car horn punctured his thoughts, returning him to the here and now. He saw a familiar red sports car pulling sharply to a parking spot. He watched as Gregory jumped out and headed across the road. He must be going to see that odious Kite fellow. He opened the car door allowing the cool air to flush across his face, invigorating his senses. He felt alive; a strength surging through his body; adrenaline pricked the hairs on his arms with gooseflesh. Gary Danvers came to a decision. His phone rang again. It was Deidrie again. He powered it off and left it on the car's front seat. From the boot of the car, he grabbed a tire iron and discreetly hid it under his coat. He lifted his collar against the weather and followed Gregory across the road.

Bill called an ambulance, not that they would be able to do

much for the poor sod laying with his head split in two. He called the murder squad, who were about ten minutes away having already been in the area and he had arrested Gerald Plimpton on suspicion of two murders. The old man hardly seemed the cold-blooded killer type but who could tell these days? Maybe he was pushed over the edge by a delay in his bin collection day or his garden gnome got broken. Gerald hadn't said much since he had vomited over Bill's shoes. He looked like he was in shock or something, Bill thought. If the stink of sick didn't come out of his shoes, Bill was going to put in a claim; fifty quid these cost him… ten years ago.

Bill walked over to the door to see if could hear the murder squad coming. They should be blues and twos-ing it here. A voice bellowed from the doorway as Gregory Danvers strode into the shop.

'Havery! We need to talk about my old man, he is getting suspicious.' He stopped short, meeting Bill's eyes. Gregory Danvers froze. His eyes lowered to the blood on the floor and then to Gerald.

'What's he suspicious about Gregory? And why is that of interest to the late Mr Kite?' asked Bill, in his most policeman of policeman's voices.

Gregory bolted… straight into the clutches of PC Pembroke, who was more than pleased to forcibly restrain Gregory Danvers on account of Danvers getting a lucky punch on him on a previous arrest. He always felt irked that Danvers hadn't been properly punished for that. A well-placed knee in Danvers's soft squishy groin area was the cherry on the cake. Gregory crumpled into a sobbing heap on the floor.

'Thank you, Pembroke,' Bill said 'Let's get these two sorted for questioning. Their workplace is just over the road. Take them there, while I wait for the crime team to secure the scene, then I will be right over.' It occurred to Bill that Gregory Danvers was expecting to see Harvey Kite alive. Probably should make note of that he thought feeling quite proud of himself, could rule him out of Kite's Murder. This thought train was derailed by the sight of

Gary Danvers angrily stomping towards the shop. As he got close Bill saw him produce a metal bar from underneath his jacket, his knuckles white as he gripped it tightly.

Bill stepped out of the doorway.

'Mr Danvers, a pleasure to see you. I am DCI Sagers. Could I ask, with respect, you put the tire iron down; on account that it might be misconstrued as a dangerous weapon?'

Gary Danvers stopped; his vacant eyes that seemed unfocused a second ago regained their piercing blue hue again as if he had woken from a trance. His stare breached Bill's normal stoic facade for the briefest of moments. His eyes then dropped to Gregory Danvers prone on the floor, handcuffed, held by a very tall police officer. Uncertainty spread across his face. He looked at the tire iron in his hand, then at Bill and then back to his son on the floor. A reflex muscle action attempted to conceal the tire iron behind his back, however, the rational brain took over and told him the jig was up; he dropped the tire iron in the road and raised his hands.

Bill handed over the Harvey Kite crime scene to the forensic team and ambled over to the offices of Danvers Insurance. He had sent Gerald, Gary and Gregory over there to be placed in separate offices to be questioned. The evening's events jumped around his brain, each vying for his immediate attention. Gary Danvers seemed to be intent on hurting someone with the tire iron, could that also mean that he expected to find Harvey Kite alive? What did Gregory mean when he said his Dad was getting suspicious? Where did Gerald fit into all this? And who is Baby G? Gerald, Gary, Gregory?

Gerald sipped the water, its water cooler chill slowly bringing him back to his senses. The police officer stood by the door, preventing him from leaving, not that he wanted to. Life had become, well, a little chaotic today. He was so far out of his comfort zone that he considered that comfort was probably sitting in a different time zone, pretending not to know him. He was not sure how he became the prime suspect in not one, but two murders; he didn't kill spiders and always used humane mouse traps. Hardly a hardened criminal. He was just boring old Gerald. He sighed, maybe he should have retired when he had the chance. The door opened and the shabby-looking detective walked in and sat opposite Gerald. He placed a folder on the table. The detective spoke first.

'I am DCI Sagers, do you have any idea why we want to talk to you?'

Bill liked to chuck the ball in their court first, you'd be amazed at what people would confess to under pressure. The Sausage Roll Guy was shockingly a classic example.

'Because I killed Harriett?' The words were left hanging in the air, soft and sad. 'I didn't mean to, I just meant to put her off me. I didn't kill Harvey; he was like that when I got there. What a way to go. Was she found in the bath?'

'Bath? What makes you think she died in the bath?' Up until this point Bill had thought this was going to be an easy arrest, however, something in the way the man spoke filled him with doubt; he didn't fit the profile.

'Well, not sure where else you would use a bath bomb. That was the gift I got. A duck-shaped bath bomb. I presume she had a reaction to it?'

'A duck-shaped bath bomb? Not a cake?' asked Bill.

'From Harvey Kite's place on the high street.' Gerald thought this was important information, but the officer's face said otherwise. 'Dazza saw it, hideous thing. He agreed that it would do the job.'

'Do the Job?', Bill asked patiently.

'I am not explaining myself at all, am I? Can we just speak to Dazza, he should still be on shift, around the other side of the building?' Gerald looked at him in earnest. Bill shrugged, what is the worst that can happen, he thought.

The body slumped prone in the office chair. Gerald, Bill and two uniformed officers stood there silently, stunned. Bill moved forward taking the wrist and attempted to find a pulse, although it was obvious from the look of the man that he wouldn't find one. He noted that the body was still warm to the touch, meaning death hadn't occurred too long ago. He noted some crumbs on the man's shirt, however, could see no sign of food. On the floor, under the desk, he spotted a mobile phone. He held it up to the man's face. The facial recognition unlocked the phone immediately, Bill felt quite proud of himself; good coppering he thought once again. The phone was on the call history screen. The last name dialled was Gerald. Bill noted the time was when Gerald was earlier in the evening, around the time he saw Gerald in the pub.

'Have you got your phone on you?', he asked Gerald. Gerald took out his phone and handed it to Bill.

'It'll need charging,' he said.

Five minutes later the screen illuminated, showing one missed call and one voicemail. Bill pressed the voicemail button and the speaker. Dazza's unmistakable, slightly nasal voice emitted from the speaker.

'Hello, mate listen...just had a thought. I think I saw Danvers switching the tags on the Secret Santa presents the other day. Thought they looked suspicious, Speak later.'

Bill looked at Gerald and then at the two officers. The taller of the two turned to the other one and handed him a five-pound note.

'Told you it would be a weird one if Bill was involved.'

Bill sighed, assessing the three men in front of him; strike why the iron is hot he thought. He was sure Gerald was innocent of any wrongdoing, just a wrong place wrong time kind of guy. The younger of the two Danvers, Gregory, had some prior run-ins with the local constabulary, however, Gary Danvers, the father, was a stand-up member of the community. Town councillor, keynote speaker at the yearly policeman's ball and even turned on the Christmas lights this year. Frustratingly, Bill thought, all three men's first names started with a G. He still had an unanswered question. Who was the mysterious BabyG on the video call with

Harriett Most? Bill was willing to lay money it was one of these men, but he didn't want to play his hand too early. Establish the facts first, he thought.

Gerald was in a daze. He was aware of the detective talking but wasn't really taking it in. Gregory Danvers was shouting angrily; Gary Danvers was threatening to sue them for bringing his good name into disrepute. Gerald felt sad that his friend was dead, he felt sad that Harriett was dead, maybe he was too unkind to her. His world felt surreal. He was brought to his senses by DCI Sagers' booming voice. It echoed off the windows of the room and silenced the quarrelling Danvers.

'Who is BabyG!'

Gerald noticed the vitriolic sneer on Gregory's face twisted into a malevolent laugh. He turned to his father.

'They got you dirty old man, bang to rights, all your perverted little secrets!'

Gerald looked at Gary, his whole body slumped, head bowed like a man defeated. Bill looked from one to the other.

'Explain?'

'I can't.' Gary said quietly. Gregory gleefully took up the story.

'Me and mum came home earlier than expected a few weeks. There he was sitting in the front room in a nappy and a dummy hanging out of his mouth. That Harriett woman was on the computer screen in her altogether. He was one of her naughty boys, Little Baby Gary. He looked pathetic. Mum was mad as hell at him and then she found out the woman was blackmailing him. A grand a month she wanted. You want a motive for murder…that is one hell of a perverted motive right there.'

The room stayed silent for a few seconds but to Gerald felt like an eternity. He looked at DCI Sagers who looked stunned. The silence was broken when the cleaning lady entered, bringing in a fresh urn of hot water, tea and some cake and left.

'I didn't hurt anyone,' Gary pleaded 'I paid up just as she asked, no fuss. Then I found it wasn't her blackmailing me. It was that Harvey Kite and that toe rag of a son of mine. They hacked her work email account and sent the damned emails from it.'

'Hacked!' interrupted Gregory, 'We had her password. Des in accounting gave it to me. It's "Tiddles" he told me, after Mrs Slocum's pussy. She was a fan, apparently. We only did it for shits and giggles; teach you a lesson. I didn't have the heart to tell Mum. She deserved to be angry at you.'

The two seemed to be about to fly at each other when the door opened. A uniformed officer entered the room.

'Sir, you might want to take a look at the CCTV footage from Sainsbury's'. It is interesting.'

Bill watched the screen. He saw Gary Danvers and Gerald at the same till. There seemed to be an exchange of words and Gerald didn't look happy.

'What am I looking at?' Bill asked.

'Take a look at what Gregory Danvers is buying; eggs, flour, butter, etcetera'

'The ingredients for a cake?' Bloody hell thought Bill, if that ain't suspicious, then I don't know what it. Gregory Danvers wasn't exactly the Mary Berry type.

'Who gave Harriet Most a cake as the Secret Santa present?' asked Bill.

The two Danvers looked at each other, quizzical looks on their faces. Bill continued.

'The dead bloke, Dazza wasn't it, he said he saw one of you switch presents. That cake then killed her. Laced with poison. I am pretty sure Dazza suffered the same fate. Poor bloke probably couldn't help himself; neither stood a chance. Now, Gregory, I got you on CCTV buying what looks like the ingredients for a cake. Might not be the strongest case but I am sure a jury would find it a mighty fine coincidence, don't you?'

Gregory swallowed hard, he almost seemed frozen. This clock in the meeting room seemed to intensify its tick. Gerald counted five ticks but it felt like five hundred.

'I-I got Dad a cake; he was my Secret Santa this year. Asked Mum to make it for me. Didn't know what else to get' said Gregory shrugging.

'No, I got a stupid duck-shaped bath bomb, irritated the hell out of my skin, and my ball sack is still red raw now.' said Gary.

'So, the gifts were swopped?' asked Bill. 'Gerald said that he got Harriett a bath bomb, didn't you?' Gerald nodded. 'Dazza said "Danvers switched the presents"; which one of you switched the presents?' Bill thumped the table for dramatic effect.

In unison the two Danvers replied, 'Well, I didn't!' Bill threw his arms up in the air in exasperation.

Something was gnawing at Gerald as he watched one of the police officers pour himself a cup of tea out of the urn. They then picked up a plate and a slice of cake and in slow motion raised it to their mouth. Cake, Gerald thought. Danvers, another thought collided with it. Dazza called all the Danvers...Danvers, even Mrs Danvers, Danvers switched the presents, she was mad as hell, Gregory Danvers himself said that...and she made the cake.

Gerald jumped up and hit the cake out of the officer's hand.

'Oi! That is striking an officer of the law', the officer objected.

'The cake, I think it is poisoned, I think it is Deidre Danvers that killed Harriett and Dazza! Possibly Harvey too!'

'Deidre?...Deidre?' Gary Danvers repeated. 'I have been married to the woman for forty years. I would know if she was a killer!'

'Dunno Dad, she was pretty angry.' Gregory said.

'Do you know where she is right now?' Bill asked.

Turned out Deidre Danvers wasn't too far away at all. She had been pushing the vacuum cleaner around outside the meeting room in a dark wig and a face mask. When she revealed herself by trying to attack her husband with a cake knife, it seemed to be all but a full confession. Bill hated to admit it, but the old bloke had beaten him to it, not with skill or finesse; just pure old dumb luck...all a good copper needs. All in all, a very odd series of events. Bill's weird list was now The Amorous Chicken Fancier, Sausage Roll Guy, Mittens and the Stew Saga and The Secret Santa Murders.

The End

FLESH AND FEATHERS

By Megan Johnson

In the foothills of the Sierra Nevada Mountains stands an estate built on gold. A creek trickles slowly across the back of the property and, in the evenings, you can hear the croaking of frogs from the last bedroom on the third floor. If you wake up early enough in the mornings when there's still dew dotting the grass, you might be lucky enough to see mule deer grazing in the field around little purple Nose skullcaps and bridal Water minerslettuce. The wind whistles across the old brown shutters in the winter. When it gets damp outside, right at the tail end of winter, the wooden floors smell like centuries of fireplace smoke and pine needles. In the living room, there are little notches carved into the corner of one of the walls. Claire thinks it's from a family marking the heights of their growing children. Every time I walk by that wall, I run my fingers along the jagged scars. Sometimes I get a splinter.

We have always lived on the Santa Estate. Claire and I were born here, in Santa Maria House, which was risky for our mother considering the closest midwife was nearly an hour's drive away; the closest *anyone* is nearly an hour's drive away. Worse than having no doctors near, we had no television, no take-out food, and no boys to gawk at in geometry. All there was to fill our minds with were sounds of braying deer and the crackling of a freshly lit fire and the first breath you take after stepping outside in January, the way it burns your lungs and freezes your nose hairs. All of it training for today, when we Change.

Today is our eighteenth birthday. September 27th, the time of year right before leaves start to color and fall to the ground, when the warm western winds still blow through on sunny days, the forest on the cusp of fall. I'm staring out of my window as the sun peeks over the treeline, the Great Pine casting its first shadow of the day, twirling a strand of long dark hair around my finger. My chin has been resting on my pillow for so long that my neck is starting to cramp. I reluctantly drag my arms out from underneath my comforter, propping myself up by the elbows until I'm sitting upright. I rub my eyes. The clock says 6:00, but it's ahead by three minutes, so I know I have some time with my thoughts before Claire comes barging through my door.

I run my hands through my hair. *Don't think, just jump. Your instincts will do the rest.* The sun is almost fully over the trees. I twist my legs out from under me and stand up on the cool floors, feeling the life of the wood through the soles of my feet. I yawn and reach my arms up in a stretch before padding over to the window and pushing the glass open. The damp morning air rushes over me and, for a moment, I am in the sky. *This is going to be the rest of my life.* As I breathe in the smell of the morning, my door creaks open, and quick little footsteps hurry behind me. A gentle hand on my shoulder. Claire.

My twin sister and I were born on a blue moon. We are two souls intertwined, Mother says. Claire is my opposite to the naked eye: her white blonde hair to my dark brown, her brown eyes to my blue, her cupid's bow gently curved to my sharp edged, her worried gaze to my steady. But on the inside, we are one, born with Shared Consciousness, a rarity in even twins born to Ancient Murder families. From the beginning, we have been connected.

But we must face our Changing alone.

Claire's quiet voice interrupts my thoughts. "We need to get dressed, Ellie. They're going to start arriving soon."

She pulls on my shoulder, so I have to turn and face her. Her eyes are swimming with glee, and I can feel the excitement pulsing through her blood, although her demeanor suggests that she's trying to hide her anticipation from me. I look at Claire in the way only sisters know as she squeezes my hand in hers. I squeeze back.

"We can do this," I whisper.

"Together," we say at the same time, smiles creeping across both of our faces as we pull each other in for our last hug before the Change. Claire's thin fingers squeeze my shoulders before we pull apart and she breezes out of my room, softly closing the door behind her. I look back towards the sun, taking in the warmth of the morning before closing the window and turning towards the long black dress hanging from my closet door.

The light catches it just right, a sheen of color moving over the ripples of black fabric: gold dust sewn into the gossamer threads. Every Changing cloth is infused with a part of the land, it's what bonds you to your Murder.

I shimmy out of my pajamas and into the dress, the fabric feels weightless and comforting, like a second skin.

A chill passes over me. Little black specks have started to creep across the horizon toward the Estate. I quickly tuck my hair behind my ears, padding over to my bedroom door. I feel Claire open her door right before I open mine, and, for a moment, we stare at each other from across the hall. Her heartbeat quickens with mine. We both know the curse of Changing twins: you can't let half a soul live. Either we both live or we both die. We walk together and meet at the top of the stairs, sucking in a deep breath, and descend to meet the Murders.

I was always good at keeping secrets.

As a girl, it was little things. Like when Claire came into my room at night, restless with worry, and we would stay up talking for hours past bedtime. Or when we snuck down to the pantry after dark and ate chocolate kisses. Or the books Father would let me borrow from the library, ones that Mother deemed "too mature."

But I'm not a girl anymore.

I'm a dedicated student of the Way. I listen with my nose and see with my ears. I can feel a storm coming from fifty miles away and I know which does are pregnant from the way they walk and I fall asleep at night with my hand against the wall, trying to feel for the pulse of life. I breathe the forest, in and out.

And despite it all, I wonder what else there is.

The world outside the Santa Estate is not alien to me. I know about the Internet and reality television shows and first dates and McDonald's. I've spent years sneaking into the kitchen at night, sliding Father's copy of the newspaper out of the trash, and reading the tiny print between smears of that night's dinner. Many nights I've stared at my ceiling, imagining a life for myself without the Murders or the Way. And a part of me yearns for it.

It's my worst and most well-kept secret. And it could very well kill us both.

All afternoon, they had been arriving in droves. First it was the Ancient Murders; they were always first. Their feet touched down in the field at Santa Maria with a lightness I had never seen before, their Transformation almost instantaneous, a cracking of bone, limbs emerging from a flurry of feathers. Their faces retain avian features, even after beaks and beady eyes sink down into soft skin.

The Original Murder sent their eldest daughter, Zarya Vorona, a tall woman who is pale as paper and just as thin. Her dark eyes hold a gaze like no other, and although her physical body takes up little space, her power is deep and old. I can feel it through the tremors of the grass. She speaks little and observes much, and she has a ruby teardrop necklace hanging from her neck, nestled at her collarbone above the collar of her dark robe.

The Ronne family sent Wendell Ronne, a stocky man with a hearty laugh. His family oversees all records, literature, and education regarding the rules and rituals of the Murders, and he carries an air of intelligence about him. He has a soft handshake but a heavy step and he smells of damp paper. When he saw Claire and me, he widened his arms and in a slight German accent said, "Ah, the Delaney twins. How I've waited for this day. I've already begun writing of you."

The Korbin family sent Fala Korbin, a woman whose soul reflects the gentleness of her name. A small yet strong woman, she speaks surely and directly. Her family, although not the oldest of them all, is the oldest in North America. They're distinct because of their pure white hair and feathers, known fondly as the family of the white ravens. Some say that their connection with the forest is deeper than even the Voronas.

The Corvus family sent Adriana Corvus, a woman known for giving birth to more sets of twins than any other woman in a Murder ever. The Corvus family has twelve children, all of them born in pairs of two, all of them surviving of their Changing. She and Mother had corresponded for months, Adriana easing Mother's worries over mine and Claire's chances.

The Ingram family sent Gideon Ingram. One of the tallest men I've ever seen (not that I've seen many men), he speaks with a deep booming voice. He has a long scar across his left eye from a confrontation with humans on the outside. When I spoke with him, my gaze flickered back and forth between his seeing and his dead eye.

As the sun sinks lower in the sky, Murders from around the continent begin arriving. I recognize some of them from when they visited Mother and Father in years past. Claire and I spend the day being passed from person to person, giving us wisdom, advice, and cautionary tales. The yard has been set up for the ritual, five chairs in a row near the base of the Great Pine – the 250-foot-tall tree that resides in the middle of the Estate's field– for the five Ancient family representatives. Dotted behind them stand high tables adorned with candles and small floral arrangements that Mother spent weeks making. I notice people hesitantly approaching Zarya Vorona, speaking to her quietly, their bodies tense as they await a response. I don't share their fear of the thin woman.

Once the first ray of the sinking sun hits the Great Pine, a hush rolls over the crowd that has gathered in the field. The five Ancients take their seats at the front of the crowd as Claire and I emerge and stand at the base of the tree. I can feel her heart racing, as she can feel mine. Together, we slow our hearts and let the dirt soak up our fears.

Zarya Vorona stands, her flowing robe swishing around her, and turns to face the crowd, "Today we are here to watch these two women become what they have always been," her usually quiet voice echoes through the silent air, a twinge of Russian accent lingering in her vowels. "We remember the Original Murder, the Ancient Voronas, who built their home in the dense forests of the Ural Mountains. Born from Olde magic, it was they who first felt the life of the soil, who heard the beating of wings high above the treetops. With their children, they became a Murder of Crows."

A murmur of respect echoes through the crowd. Claire's breath catches as Zarya Vorona turns to us, dark eyes piercing through the evening light.

We step forward and begin to recite the rules of the Way, "The job of every Murder is to listen to the forest, the land, the water. We are responsible for our region, for protecting it from harm and healing its wounds."

My voice quavers, but Claire's holds strong as we take another step towards the towering Great Pine. "We must fully trust in Nature and be truly courageous to fulfill our duties. If either pillar falters, our Murder could fail the forest."

I lift my foot off the ground, every millimeter abandoning what could have been. "The existence of the Murders must be kept hidden from the rest of the world. Only in secret can they operate successfully and bring true balance and justice to the land. The world outside of our forest can be tempting from above, but we must place our responsibility before our own desires."

We sink to our knees, eyes raised to the sky, the setting sun getting ever lower. My thin dress damp with the evening dew, I feel the heart of the forest thumping beneath me.

The sound of ripping flesh and the soft beating of wings makes me shiver. I hope everyone assumes my goosebumps are from the cool evening air.

As the bottom edge of the sun hits the treeline, I hear a flurry of wings beating, suddenly gasping out in pain as thick claws sink into my shoulders. Warm blood trickle down my arms as I'm lifted into the air, higher and higher, my body rocking with every flap of wings.

As we reach the top of the Great Pine, the claws loosen their grip, dropping me down on a thick branch where I rest, crouching, catching my breath. I hear Claire's bodyweight thump down, and look to my right, where she stands up, a steady hand trailing the thick trunk of the tree, dried blood crusting at her shoulders. The two birds – eagles, I realize – that carried us up linger in the air, a look of longing in their small eyes, blood drying on their talons. I hear Claire gasp, putting a hand gently up to her mouth. My heart pangs as I know what she knows: Mother and Father.

They hover with us for another moment, but not any longer, before diving down to rejoin the crowd below.

A silence settles over the air, and I straighten my legs, standing up and meeting Claire's eyes across the trunk. I feel her reaching out to me in her mind, and I reach back. We calm each other, letting the wind whisk away our fears, letting the weathered branches of the Great Pine hold the burden of our lives, before pushing each other out of our minds. We must do this alone.

I look down at the crowd in front of Santa Maria, and then up and out towards the forest. I can finally see the tops of the trees and not just their silhouettes in the sky. The clouds swirl in the east, a storm brewing. The endlessness of the sky holds me tightly; I have to remember to breathe. Life pulses through the branch below my bare feet, hundreds of years of life and tradition all in one place.

And as the sun dips below the horizon and the sky darkens, my feet push off from the branches of the Great Pine. I hurtle towards the earth in slow motion, hands pointed down in front of me, the Murders in the field mere specks of life below. Cold buffets my face, my long hair trailing behind me. I hear the grass whistle in the breeze, the first coolness of the night air pulses through my lungs. As I fall farther and farther, my senses heighten. I can hear a fly buzzing near Gideon Ingram's face, I can feel the rapid heartbeat of a rabbit burrowing away from a coyote, I taste the evening dew on my lips. My bones crack.

I am the deer braying in the field, my thick sides rising and falling with each breath, clouds of steam puffing out of my nose. I am the frog croaking by the creek and the water flowing over the rocks. I am the rocks. I am the cold winter wind, whistling over the shutters and rattling the glass panes. I am a patch of Nose skullcaps poking out of the soil in the spring, reaching for sunlight and life. I am the old wood waiting to be burned and the new sapling growing its first leaf. I am the morning dew and the low-hanging clouds. I am a fire ripping through the trees and a thunderclap that scatters the sparrows. I am the worm and the mouse and the fox and the mushroom. I am the first snowfall and the last day of summer. I am the flesh and the feathers and the air between them.

YOU'D BETTER WATCH OUT

By Mandy Kerr

Paul flicked a switch cutting off Noddy Holder just as he was building up to his rasping crescendo of *Merry Christmas Everybody.*

'Thank Christ for that.' He closed his eyes, rocked back in his chair and swung his legs up on the desk.

'Looks like you're on your own tonight mate, Vince has rung in sick again. Maybe he's got caught in the storm, struck by lightning or something. Hangoveritis more likely.'

Andy shook his head and turned to the bank of monitors in front of Paul.

'Lightweight. He's gonna have to watch it though, he's already on a warning. I doubt his missus is going to be too pleased if he gets sacked just before Christmas.'

He scanned the screens. The deserted shopping centre lay spread before him like four spokes of a wheel with the information desk at its hub. By day it was the beating heart of the mall, where friends met and lost children were consoled with lollipops until they were reunited with their frantic parents. Andy relished the sense of power he felt when he manned the control room at night. He was the brain, the nerve centre, and even while the shopping centre slept, he controlled its basic functions. The omnipotence was almost overwhelming at times. Since bailing out of the army he had spent a couple of years recuperating before finding this job that appealed to his sense of routine and discipline. Opting for the night shift gave him time to be alone and think without the hordes of marauding shoppers. 'Self-care' his therapist had called it. Andy preferred to think of it as self-preservation. Of course, Shirley hadn't been too keen on the hours at first, but once she'd seen his first pay packet she'd soon come round to his way of thinking. It was funny how the promise of a holiday to Mauritius could do that.

'Right mate, I'd better get out there. Once more into the breach and all that.'

Paul tossed him a walkie-talkie.

'Don't forget that and watch out for Scrooge's ghost.'

'Scrooge wasn't a ghost you idiot, like Frankenstein wasn't a monster.'

'Yeah, yeah, whatever. Stay safe out there Andy lad.' Paul grinned.

Andy left the control room and headed downstairs. Keying in the code on the security pad, he let himself into the shopping centre. As always, he felt a frisson of pleasure at being the only person in the normally crowded space. A sepulchral hush enveloped him as he stood by the information desk and surveyed the shop-lined avenues radiating outwards. Behind the desk, a panoramic lift reached upwards to the first floor and two escalators flanked a towering artificial Christmas tree, its bulbs now extinguished. By the tree, a gaudily painted wooden hut sat on a carpet of artificial snow, its roof draped in cotton wool and tinsel. 'Santa's Grotto' proclaimed a sign over the door, 'Meet Santa and his elves. A gift for every child. Only £5!' Andy smiled to himself as he thought of the specific elf he would most like to meet, a pretty young thing called Jenny who wore those green tights in a very fetching manner and somehow managed to make pointed ears and a floppy hat look sexy. He sighed. Shirley was bringing the kids tomorrow, maybe he should join them and get in a bit of festive flirting with Jenny the elf. A bit of 'elf care.' He sniggered.

Andy laid his walkie-talkie on the desk and gave it a spin. North, south, east or west? Which to start with tonight? He watched as the antenna slowly stopped spinning at the west-facing avenue and set off in that direction, his shoes squeaking on the polished floor. By day, the mall was brightly lit with hundreds of overhead lights, but at night only the emergency lighting was in use and every few metres creamy bulbs created soft puddles of illumination which punctuated the gloom. Swathes of foil Christmas stars, snowflakes and reindeer were strung high across the walkways. Their normal shiny, twinkling displays which moved in the draft of the air conditioning, were now a series of deformed shadows which stretched across the floor like fingers. Andy shuddered as if those fingers were scraping up his spine. Like they sometimes did when he was lying awake in his sweat-soaked bed, staring at the ceiling trying not to scream.

He carried on past the shop fronts glancing inside each one as he passed. Once he had found a customer banging on the window of Urban Outfitters. The young guy had tried his first taste of skunk after an afternoon in the pub, decided to buy a pair of jeans and passed out in the changing room just before closing time. The staff member responsible for locking up that day had been in a hurry to leave and had neglected to check the store properly. It was the kind of mistake you only ever made once Andy thought. He paused at the window of H.Samuel. A display of diamond rings sparkled among the tinsel. Maybe he should think about making an honest woman of Shirley at last? They had two kids together after all and let's face it, he probably wasn't going to be getting any better offers. Not at his age and not with 'his issues' as she liked to refer to his condition. A blast of static burst from his walkie talkie startling Andy away from his thoughts.

'Paul, that you mate? Everything ok?'

Silence. Andy pressed the receiver to his ear. He sensed that the channel was open and that someone was there. Listening. Paranoia's going to annoy ya. He snorted uneasily.

'Stop messing with me Paul, you're not funny.'

Another buzz of static, louder this time, hissed into his ear and he dropped the walkie-talkie as if it was a live snake. It clattered onto the floor and slid into the shadow of the shop doorway.

'For fuck's sake.'

Andy bent towards it. A deafening explosion of thunder reverberated around him, accompanied by a flash of lightning so bright it seemed to sear a negative image of the shop window onto his retinas. Christ, that storm must be bad. Moisture gathered on his top lip and he swiped it away.

Amir. Andy hadn't thought of that name for years but suddenly it was rolling around in his brain poking at his synapses, prying open firmly sealed memory banks. A conversation they had shared in Helmand Province on Christmas Day 2009 slammed into his head front and centre. He remembered back to Operation Panther's Claw when he had been deployed as part of the 26th Royal Artillery Regiment to assist in training Afghani soldiers. He and Amir had bonded over a shared love of football and passion for Manchester United in particular. They had got their hands on some illicit booze and were toasting their families. Talk had turned to festive traditions and how as a child Andy had hung up a stocking and left out mince pies and sherry for Santa, plus a carrot for Rudolph.

'Of course, you had to make sure you were on the nice list rather than the naughty list!'

'And what would happen if you were naughty child?'

'Well, nothing, you'd still get your presents, it was just to try to make you behave, you know?'

'Why you behave if you know you get presents? Adults in my village of Nurgal scare children with stories of Ghor Baba. He is powerful man with lightning powers, that take naughty children away from their mothers and fathers to place called Ghori Baibani.' Amir's fingers strayed to a talisman around his neck which he rubbed distractedly.

'And you believed that?'

'Yes of course. We behaved very well. If not, Ghor Baba, he come. Ghori Baibani is not a place you want to go.'

'But it's just a story, right? Like Santa?'

'Ah you say that Andy but let me tell you time when I was small boy. Ali, boy from my village, very bad boy, he torment chickens and steal bread. Then laugh. Laugh, always he laugh. Never sorry. One night a big storm came. The sky flashing as bright as day. Flash, flash, flash. Ali, he disappear. We look and look. Everyone in village look. But Ali gone and never come back. I did not tell my father what I saw but I tell you now Andy. I saw Ghor Baba. In flash of light I saw tall, tall shape walking like a man but not man. He had sack on his back which wriggled like when Ali threw bag of kittens into river. I saw the eyes of Ghor Baba yellow like the sun and flashing like the storm. I run home faster than cheetah and hide in my bed. I swear by Allah what I say is true, I would not lie to you my friend.'

Then they had toasted some more with the remaining alcohol, but the atmosphere in the tent had grown oppressive and Andy had not slept well that night. He had seen the way Amir had sought comfort in the protective force of the amulet and the conviction in his eyes. The next day, Boxing Day, Amir had been hit by a Taliban grenade launcher and was identified only by his bloody talisman. Andy carried the guilt of that day still. He had let Amir down. His rational self knew that was ridiculous, no amount of training could have avoided what happened, but guilt was not always a rational emotion, and it was equally irrational to feel none at all at some of the atrocities he had committed.

IT'S CHRISTMAS!

Music blasted from the speakers in the shopping centre, jerking Andy away from the stifling, dusty tent. Slade at full volume. Andy grabbed at his walkie-talkie, his hands shaking, his grip slippery.

'Paul, what are you doing? Do you think this is funny? Switch the fucking music off!'

Are you hanging up your stocking on the wall?

'Turn it off! You're not scaring me. I'm fucking leaving if you don't stop it.'

There was no answer. No crackle. No static fuzz. Just dead air.

Andy ran back to the information desk and pressed his forehead to the cold, hard surface. Sweat dripped onto the marble-effect Formica. Ghor Baba is not real. He's like Santa or the Tooth Fairy or the Easter Bunny. The bullets were real, the blood was real, the screaming was real. The sights and the sounds and the smells were real. But Ghor Baba is not real.

'Right Paul, I warned you, I've had enough, I'm off home. Fuck your job.'

Andy heard the unsteadiness in his voice and imagined Paul, up in the control room, feet on the desk, hand on the volume knob, laughing his arse off at his colleague's panic. He tossed the impotent walkie-talkie onto the desk. Maybe he'd come back to work too soon, maybe he hadn't been as ready as his therapist thought. He flicked the rubber band on his wrist and tried to focus on his breathing. In and out. Nice and slow. Controlled. A mechanical grinding noise snapped Andy's head up. The lift started to move slowly upwards, its transparent capsule gleaming dully in the emergency lighting. He groped under the desk and flipped open the control panel feeling in the dim light for the main power switch to the lift. It was set to the off position. He toggled it up and down. Maybe it was a fuse? Maybe a power surge from the storm? Maybe...? He couldn't hear himself think with the damn music thundering out.

I hope you're having fun.

The lift ground to a halt on the first floor and its doors opened. Andy gazed up at it, open-mouthed as if expecting all the demons from hell to start pouring out. The doors closed again. No demons, so that was a bonus. He felt a bubble of hysteria bulging within him. What was going on? He was actually relieved that there were no demons running amok in the shopping centre? He took a deep breath. Deep, cleansing breaths were as good as medication according to his therapist. What did she know anyway? She hadn't experienced what he had. A broken nail was probably as much as she'd had to cope with. Andy's bubble of hysteria burst into laughter which erupted out of him like a lanced boil.

Look to the future now.

The music stopped, leaving in its place a thundering silence. Andy slumped over the desk, his pulse pounding in his ears, an erratic soundtrack to his heart. Just breathe. It's not hard. In and out. Nice and slow. The adrenaline which had crashed over his body like a breaking wave, gradually subsided leaving him beached and exhausted. His uniform shirt clung damply to his back as he straightened up and reached for his walkie-talkie, his hand trembling. He wondered why he wasn't at home with Shirley sharing a bottle of wine and a takeaway. He could do a lot worse. He thought of the kids, tucked up warmly in bed and was overcome with a desire to be there with them. They weren't bad kids really although Kyle could be a bit of a handful at times. Maybe their visit to Santa's grotto tomorrow would distract him for a bit and the incentive of a present would keep him off the naughty list. Even if just for a little while.

He walked slowly towards the door marked *Staff Only* already planning in his head the ear bashing he was going to give Paul. The bastard deserved everything he had coming. A faint rustling sound stopped him dead in his tracks. He stood and listened. There it was again. It sounded like an animal moving through undergrowth, through sun-bleached grass as brittle as straw. Andy felt the tickle of hairs on the back of his neck standing to attention. It was coming from behind him, from near the desk. He turned and edged towards the looming Christmas tree, his senses on high alert. The rustling came again. The wooden grotto? He remembered that there was straw inside, part of a tableau of farm animals consisting of over-stuffed sheep and a mangy looking donkey. Not mice again surely? They'd only just had the pest controller round to deal with a minor infestation. The straw would make a perfect nest for rodents looking to get in from the storm. Dear God, not rats, it certainly sounded too big to be a mouse. Andy cautiously approached the doorway of the grotto, his walkie-talkie grasped like a club in his hand. A curtain of forest green velvet hung across the doorway. He gingerly pulled it to one side with trembling fingers and stepped into the shadows.

In the shopping centre, once more empty and silent, garlands of baubles and foliage gently swayed and spun in the sterile air, casting shadows that moved like deformed fingers across the floors and across the reflections in shop windows. The glossy paint of the grotto glowed orange against the carpet of artificial snow on which it stood, turning it to sand. A bright spear of lightning lit up the space through the skylights in the roof and in the depths of the wooden hut eyes as yellow as the sun flashed as brightly as the storm.

It's only just begun.

Printed in Great Britain
by Amazon

38277483R00030